LERA AUERBACH AND MARILYN NELSON

A is for Oboe

The Orchestra's Alphabet

illustrated by

PAUL HOPPE

DIAL BOOKS FOR YOUNG READERS

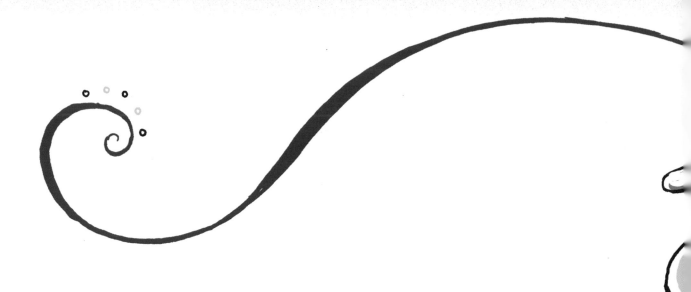

A The oboe insists that he can't
adjust his tuning to anyone else.
Everyone has to tune to him:
He won't play if he doesn't get his way.
That's why the first note you hear
as you take your seat in the concert hall
is a stubborn oboe playing his **"A."**
And then the whole orchestra tuning in.

B Presenting the **bassoon**, the orchestra's grandpa,
complaining impatiently through his nose.
And the contrabassoon, with a voice so low
it makes you hear roots growing in the woods.

C Striding onstage with a magic baton,
followed by a force field of attention,
the **conductor** doesn't play. (And don't ask her to sing!)
She waves her hands, filling the air with vibration.
Like the captain on the bridge of a great ship,
she navigates the **composer**'s musical charts.

The baton summons the mellow **clarinets**,
whose voices range from soprano to bass.
The clarinets can croon or leap,
make you cry, sigh, or boogie in your seat.

D The world's oldest instrument is the **drum**.
Drums have existed since the birth of humankind,
palpitating, counting off life's seconds.
Drums can thunder, roar, or whisper.
And some prefer to be called timpani.
(They get upset if anyone calls them drums.)

E The **English horn**, or *cor anglais*,
is neither English nor a horn.
A bit confused about his name,
the oboe's big brother used
to be addressed as "Angel's Horn."
But he's no angel. Melancholy, proud,
he's a philosopher whose velvet truths
embrace us with our own unspoken want.

F What is an orchestra without a **flute**?
Or several. And at least one piccolo,
whose shrill trills lilt, filling the ear with thrills.
She's tiny, but fierce: a ninja Tinker Bell.

G Musical instruments aren't "things" but "beings":
musicians call them "he" or "she."
Each instrument has its own character,
its mind, its moods and caprices.
Violin and viola: "she"?
Contrabass: always "he"? What of cello?
And what about the mysterious,
gender-bending **glockenspiel**?

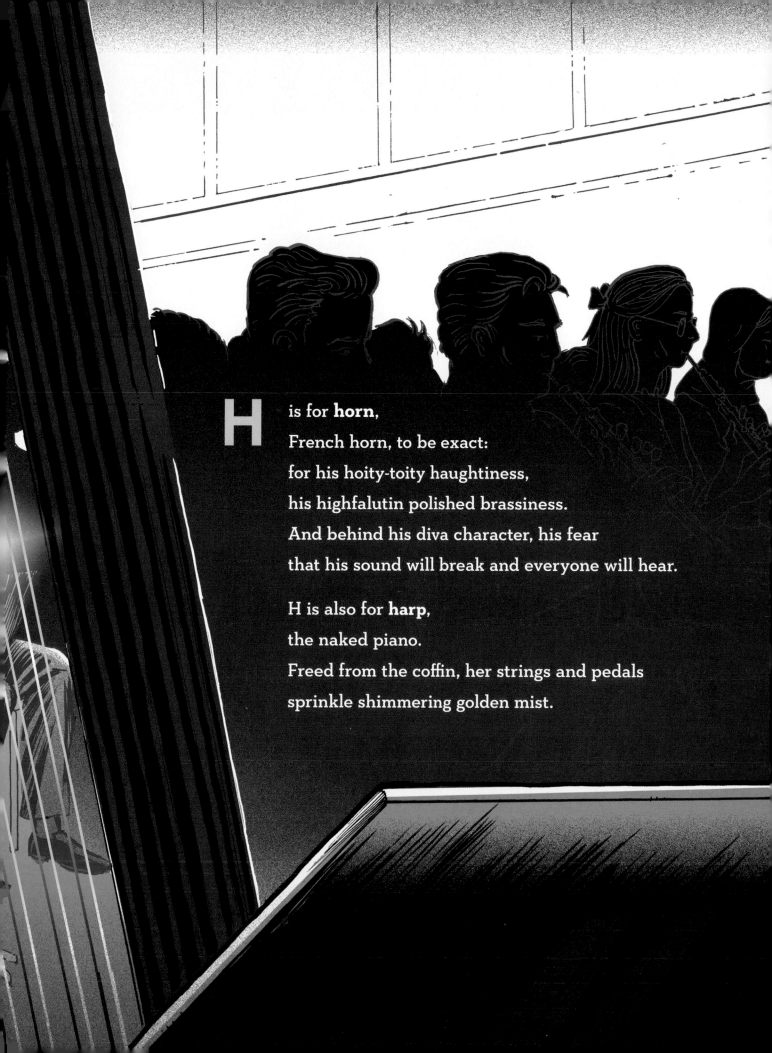

H is for **horn**,
French horn, to be exact:
for his hoity-toity haughtiness,
his highfalutin polished brassiness.
And behind his diva character, his fear
that his sound will break and everyone will hear.

H is also for **harp**,
the naked piano.
Freed from the coffin, her strings and pedals
sprinkle shimmering golden mist.

I is . . . I. Meaning you or I:
the people who go to the concert.
We sit sometimes dazzled, sometimes puzzled,
sometimes mesmerized by the musicians,
and grateful to the composers who conjured
and wrote the thousands of little black notes
the musicians play, to ignite in us
chrysanthemums of neural fireworks.

J **Jazz** is a language musicians speak
in seamlessly eloquent grooves.
Jazz is spontaneity in a frame,
instruments playing yes at the same time.
Jazz proves people can think to each other,
communicate telepathically without a word.
Jazz grins, sharing a fist bump of rhythm.
Jazz slaps palms in a musical high five.

Keyboards make sounds in many ways.
Pianos, organs, celestas, harpsichords
strike hammers on strings or chimes,
or whoosh air into pipes
to roar or pluck, prickle like porcupines,
or lift us like a one-winged Pegasus
with black and white keys to delight,
unlock, and open the gates of wonderment.

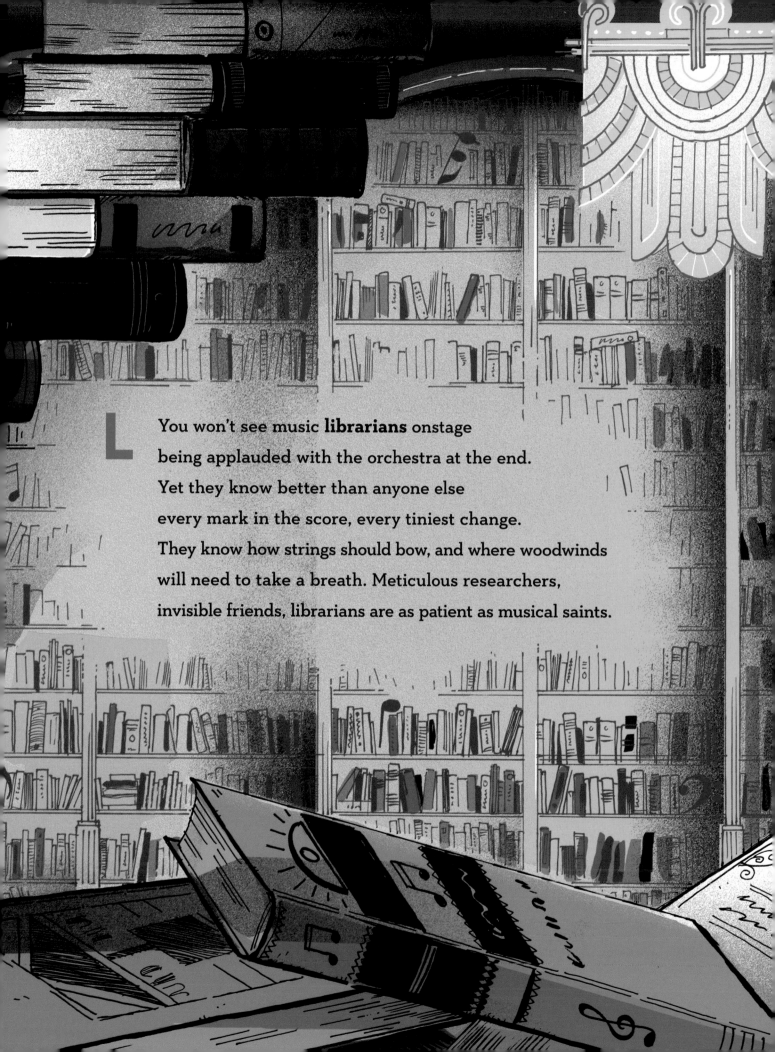

L You won't see music **librarians** onstage
being applauded with the orchestra at the end.
Yet they know better than anyone else
every mark in the score, every tiniest change.
They know how strings should bow, and where woodwinds
will need to take a breath. Meticulous researchers,
invisible friends, librarians are as patient as musical saints.

M M for the musical phrase, always in **motion**.
Each **motif** has its gravity center,
like the eyes of a portrait.
M for the **metronome**, musician's helper.
And for **meter**: boxcars in the freight train
of time that carries **melodies** soaring.
For **music** itself. But what is music?
Is it the very breath of everything alive?

N With no music **notation**, no scores could exist.
With no scores, there would be no orchestra.
Some songs might be remembered and passed down,
but history would be void of symphonies.
Human music, like birdsong in the spring,
would be scintillation tossed to the four winds.

The **orchestra** makes one out of many:
a diverse family of musicians
weaves with instruments of wood and metal
a many-colored tapestry of sounds.
They read each other's minds and make
the turn of a phrase together
as gracefully as a flock of starlings
painting evening skies with murmuration.

Percussionists are magicians,
witches, wizards, jugglers, casters of spells.
Out of many ingredients
they transform touch to miracle.
They bring fire with cymbals.
They release sparks with vibraphone.
They frighten with gongs, impress with bass drum,
dance us away with marimba.
They control a rainbow. They scatter spice.
(Here, for good measure, a triangle's ding.)

Q All parts in a symphony have their Qs.
Or **cues**. They are navigational clues.
Cue notes are the quotations on the page
of notes played by others while you wait
for the time to start playing your line.
Cue notes are Hansel's breadcrumbs, your way
out of the woods. They're Ariadne's thread,
leading you through the labyrinth of the score.

R R is **frrrrrrrrulato** in brass and woodwinds.
Musicians make it by rrrrrrrrolling their tongues.
Their notes can trrrrrremolo, flutterrrrrr, or grrrrrrrowl,
or rrrrrrripple like a distant waterrrrrrrfall.

R is also for **rests**. But rests in music
are never restful. They **rhythmically** burn,
they pause without stopping. They accentuate.
Their silence can be unbearably loud.

S Playing a **solo** in a **symphony**
means each note you play will be heard.
The orchestra will listen. People can tell.
This is your chance to express the music
in your interpretation, your own voice.
It's your solo. Don't tiptoe around it!

T for **tempo**: the pulse of **time**.
It is music's essential vital sign,
the heartbeat saying music is alive.

The proud brass, **trumpets**, **tuba**, and **trombones**,
shine as if they're clad in golden armor.
When they speak, their voices are resolute.

U The conductor waits for perfect stillness.
The conductor's hand is raised.
The music's heartbeat begins in silence.
In this upbeat, the orchestra opens its wings,
ready for the downbeat to let it fly.
Upbeat: a caught breath of waiting.

V **Violins, violas, violoncelli**
(and don't forget the **voluptuous** bass):
the strings are at the core of orchestration
and can spiral you beyond time and space.
The first chair violin is the concertmaster,
the orchestra's leader, second in charge.
He choreographs how the bows will dance.
Stroked with horsehair or plucked by hand,
the strings set up **vibrations** in frequencies
that sympathetically resonate with our hearts.

W Stay curious and open to the new.
Don't be content to listen only
to masterpieces by the same few
great decomposing composers.
The orchestral masterworks of our age
are being **written** now. Discover them.
Through music by a living composer,
you may cross the threshold into **wonder**.

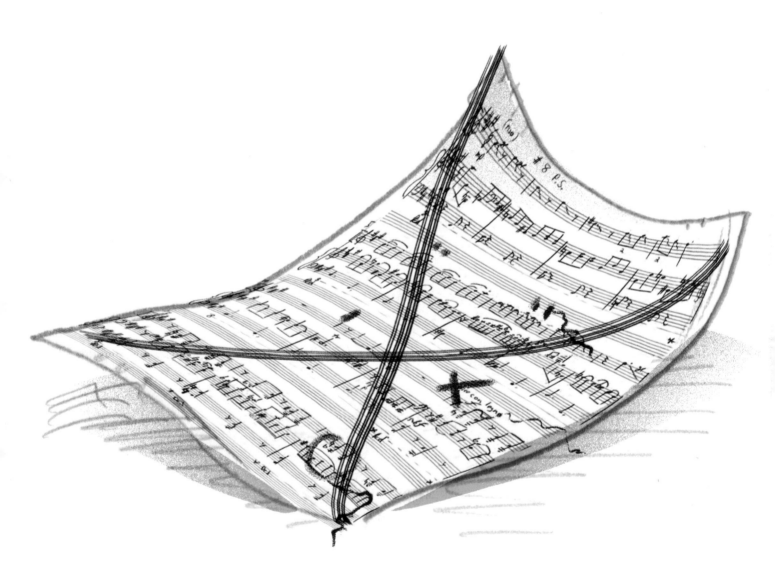

X **X** is a cut from the score. The skipped notes bleed,
considered nonessential and bypassed,
while the composer, restless in his grave
(if he be dead), moans in *trouble* clef.

Beneath the surface of those unplayed notes
sleep forgotten ecstasies.

Y is for **yes**! Y is for **you**.
Listening is a process of co-creation,
your imagination engaged to the fullest extent.
In a concert, as you listen,
you participate in the performance.
All of your memories, your reveries,
everything that has made you you
resonates and amplifies what you hear.

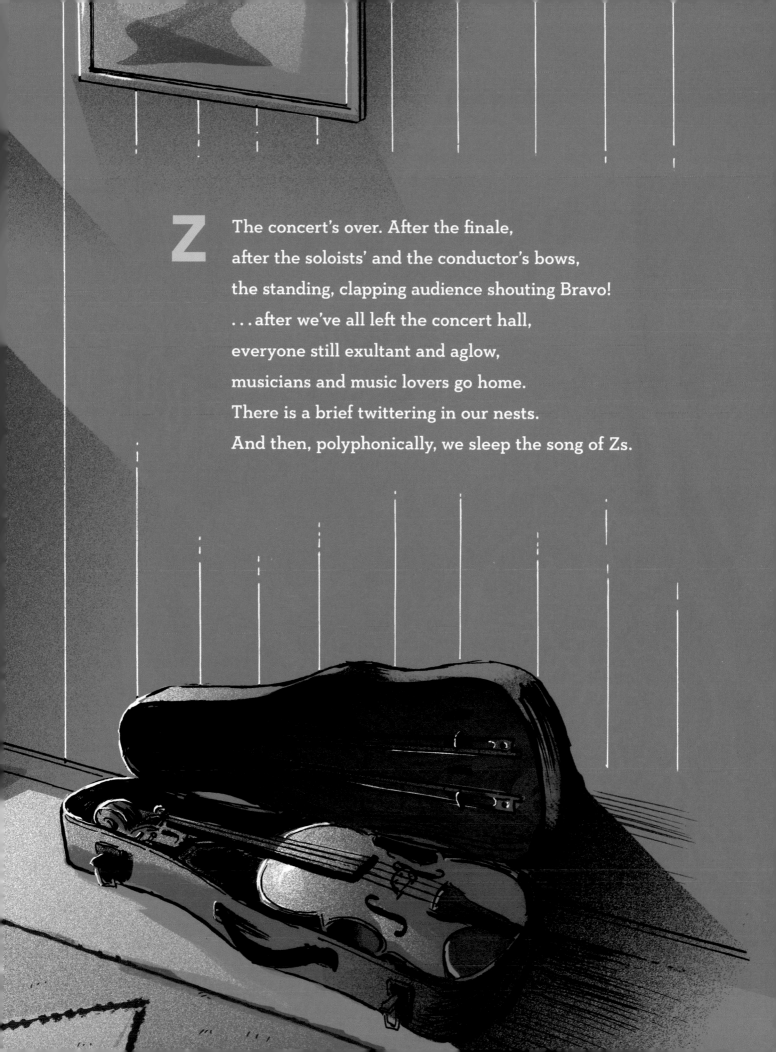

Z The concert's over. After the finale,
after the soloists' and the conductor's bows,
the standing, clapping audience shouting Bravo!
. . . after we've all left the concert hall,
everyone still exultant and aglow,
musicians and music lovers go home.
There is a brief twittering in our nests.
And then, polyphonically, we sleep the song of Zs.

To all the symphonies waiting to be born,
To all the harmonies still silent,
And to all those who will compose, perform, and love them.
—L.A. & M.N.

For my friend Jen Hill

With thanks to ShinYeon Moon

—P.H.

DIAL BOOKS FOR YOUNG READERS

An imprint of Penguin Random House LLC, New York

First published in the United States of America by Dial Books for Young Readers,
an imprint of Penguin Random House LLC, 2021

Text copyright © 2021 by Lera Auerbach and Marilyn Nelson

Illustrations copyright © 2021 by Paul Hoppe

Visit us online at penguinrandomhouse.com.

Library of Congress Cataloging-in-Publication Data is available.

Manufactured in China | ISBN 9780525553779

1 3 5 7 9 10 8 6 4 2

HH

Design by Jason Henry | Text set in Neutraface and Avenir

The artwork for this book was created with ink on paper and digital colors.